AF658279

Evincepub Publishing

Evincepub Publishing
Nehru Nagar, Bilaspur, Chhattisgarh 495001
First Published by Evincepub Publishing 2021
Copyright © Imtiyaz ahmed shah (Rahil) 2021
All Rights Reserved.
ISBN: 978-93-5446-212-2

This book has been published with all reasonable efforts taken to make the material error-free after the consent of the author. No part of this book shall be used, reproduced in any manner whatsoever without written permission from the author, except in the case of brief quotations embodied in critical articles and reviews. The Author of this book is solely responsible and liable for its content including but not limited to the views, representations, descriptions, statements, information, opinions and references ["Content"]. The Content of this book shall not constitute or be construed or deemed to reflect the opinion or expression of the Publisher or Editor. Neither the Publisher nor Editor endorse or approve the Content of this book or guarantee the reliability, accuracy or completeness of the Content published herein and do not make any representations or warranties of any kind, express or implied, including but not limited to the implied warranties of merchantability, fitness for a particular purpose. The Publisher and Editor shall not be liable whatsoever for any errors, omissions, whether such errors or omissions result from negligence, accident, or any other cause or claims for loss or damages of any kind, including without limitation, indirect or consequential loss or damage arising out of use, inability to use, or about the reliability, accuracy or sufficiency of the information contained in this book.

THE STORMING NIGHT

the night which brings mother and son to the world of truth.

Imtiyaz ahmed shah (Rahil)

DISCLAIMER

This is a work of fiction. Names, characters, business, events and incidents are the products of the author's imagination. Any resemblance to actual persons, living or dead, or actual events is purely coincidental. With this story, the author does not intend to hurt any person, religion or any relation. It's all fictional and characters are presented in such a way that they can do complete justice to the story.

AKNOWLEGMENT

I want to thank my parents and beloved friends to believe in me that I can complete this first book of my life, but most importantly I want to thank my father that he encourages me and always there to help me in finding me from the worst to the best, I can proudly say he is the greatest father ever. And a big thanks to my publishers and readers who are there to make my every book a great tool to achieve something big in life. Love you all and thanks.

TABLE OF CONTENT

THE FIGHT WHICH IS NOT RIGHT

"I don't believe in those stupid theories" my words that are filled with anger got echoed throughout the house.

She was in tears and after looking straight within my eyes for 5 minutes with silence, like she was scanning my soul for guilt, she left.

My mother Merry was gone.

It was Friday's evening and my mother wants me to be with her in the mosque and then in church also on the upcoming Sunday.

My mother and father were not of the same religion. He was a very good person but this religion thing eats him up and many of his own caste people killed him for loving my mother.

She still uses to go to the mosque for praying for my father's soul, though she was not allowed inside of the holy place that's why I am the only one who can do the tradition for him. I don't understand my mother that why she still prayed to God and believe in these damm religions.

WAIT!!! Don’t think that mother’s side is of the angels. They also tried to murder my mother but they missed it. MY mother and I were left by my father to this cruel non-sense tradition-seeking world who worships the moon and the sun but neglect their own daughter and sons.

I don't care about this world at all, but I do care about the people living in it, we as human beings focused too much on the future and past that we forget what we have in present.

A famous line from one of my favourite movies **"Yesterday is history, Tomorrow is a mystery but today is a Gift. That’s why it's called Present"**.

All of these self-claimed good people think about their ancestors like they do everything right and that they are gods, but if our ancestors can do everything right then there should be no wars, no racism, no sexism, no misogyny, and nothing bad at all from the very begging. We must understand this bitter truth that most of our ancestors are uneducated and we can say foolish also to give a push to the tradition that really doesn’t matter at all.

The harsh reality that we don’t expect, but we have to accept.

But this cannot be happening in one day, it has to happen day by day, even if you are one among the other 4300 religions of the world and thinking that *in my religion sun is not the god, we have a profit or this or that and we are different from other religions*. Sad news for you, you are also one of them because it is not about whom you worship but about whom you neglect.

If other than ethics you are worshiping a building, a book, or a name of a person born 2000 or 20000000 years ago then, you are in the religion trap bro/sis/GF/mother.

My mother merry was gone without me for praying in mosque. Every Friday I was the one she goes with and we both pray for my father's soul. I don't know how praying of ours can benefit him in the long forever afterlife run but we do that kind of stuff regularly, but not today. Today we fought on this religious topic and this one is a damm huge fight. I called her belief stupid and non-sense, even if she knew that that was the same thinking of mine about religions all the time, still hearing these words from my mouth was a shock to her.

just 30 minutes ago we both are shouting at each other about how these traditions are not of logic and just for the sake of our non-seen gods, we both are fighting and defending our ends and suddenly she got silenced. I know from her look that this time she got hurt. She left the small house of ours and then came back, I thought she wants me to come with her to the Mosque and I will be going to say a big

NO, but she only forgets about her purse and just collect it and left. This was the first time in 9 years that she didn't take me to the Mosque.
In my mind: "I crossed a line this time"

I questioned her beliefs, but more importantly, I questioned her hope. As human beings, we just can't accept this truth that we are just dust to this huge universe, and we are nothing compare to this cosmos. We made false identities in this world for us as a hope. As the old saying goes "one can live without food but cannot without hope". This time I questioned her hope. Or be precise? I damage it.
It's just like saying to a child that he cannot do the things he wants the most because of that or this, any kind of wordy weapon to murder his hope. We make things and break things and break people also in the hope for a better future. Either it's you or me we cannot live without hope and that's why it's most important for us.

I know she was sad and so as I, after regretting my actions for almost 4 minutes I went for TV and all the channels were out of network, all other than news.

**NEWS: All people of Vista area, be alert!!! A huge storm is coming [Breaking News] **

This is our residence, for a second my heart got pounded but then I just got relaxed about thinking that it can't be a very big deal.

I was in a single-bedroom house with a lobby attached to it. From the front door, if open anyone can get a glimpse of our bedroom in which there is just a double-size bed, with a bookshelf in right, a small study table in the left, and a TV hanging on the front of the bed to get a clear view.

After switching off the video box, I walk towards the lobby which has 4 chairs and a medium size dining table in the side center of the left side. A kitchen of 10 by 12 feet is attached to the side of it with a washing sink in it. I sat down on the chair for a very important and private ritual of mine.

Pubg

For the other 20 to 30 minutes, I was on my phone playing Pubg (online game) with my online friends and got a chicken dinner at it, but after more than 30 minutes I got a bit worried about my mother. Meanwhile, the speed and voice of storming wind add a flavor to this mental turmoil.

And suddenly the electricity is gone; this is a dangerous Sign because no matter what, our area never let the electricity escape, it can live without food maybe, but electricity is our area's fictional oxygen.

As a phycology student, I keep my nerves under control till now but the situation was getting a bit more serious.
I took my jacket and move towards the front door while thinking about how to make her angry mood stable and make her smile again, I was thinking about taking some chocolates for her but then remembered about her health condition. I was in confusion about where to find her, oh yes, obviously in the mosque?
The door opened and she was there standing in front of me.
"Are you ok son, I heard about the storm, and where the hell you think you are going young man, stay home and stay safe" she said these words with a serious angry babyface mixed with a caring tone in it.

I literally feel sorry for her and a bit angry with myself; it was like my brain told me to feel that way for making my mother sad even after she cared about me. A scientific fact is that a mother's unconditional love is only for her child, but I never took that seriously, until now.

We are having this moment of ours and suddenly, a bolt of huge lightning came from the sky with a loud sound, and this was just the begging of this night.

The wind starts driving crazy. The walls can hardly block the sound of the wind like they both were doing sumo wrestling at that time; the doors and windows were the witness and victims of that turmoil; they were shaking rapidly like a person who is fond of living in the Sahara Desert and is suddenly now teleported to Arctic Circle.

We both are looking at each other trying to understand the situation around us, and suddenly another lighting strikes.

I can see and feel how my mother was horrified by that course of action nature does on us, her eyes were flicking at the rate of a tesla's engine and her hands were on the way to get up in the air for prayer. Maybe her mind was too much terrified by what was happening around us.

The wind was doing its job of pounding our hearts out but maybe she needs help, and that's where the rain came into action.

Commonly here in our area Rain needs a minimum of 5 minutes to get a pace like this but today they were at it in just some fractions of a second; maybe the upload speed of nature's water department gets a boast today.

The raindrops were getting started to had a noisy party on our roof. The light was already gone but we can see each other because of the thundering, at the other second clouds also took over that territory and now we are blind too, and there was again lighting, and this was a big one; it shaped like a baby is trying to make a curve and end up making silly lines in spite.

Flashed before my eyes just for a second.

My mother and I can see each other's horrified faces because of that, and the sound of that lighting was like a meteor hits the ground.

And I was thinking *"is this the end of our lives"? *

STARTING OF NIGHT

The light was too much dense for me and very dangerous to be seen by naked eyes. Merry; my mom and I were under the same roof and were frightened to even speak, at that time I was stunned and terrified but I cannot let that fear be seen on my face, cause if I did it will break my mother also. It's not liked a Man cannot afraid, but what I am concerned about is that that she was much more frightened than me and I was the only one there to make her feel safe.

A mother makes her child felt safe and comfortable in the early days of the baby's life, she feeds her/him. It is our rightful duty to do the same when they need us, if not physically then at least mentally nurture her.

A great author once said- "the circumstances will not break you or make you, they are there just to reveal you the real you"
My mother was in hurry to find the candles, "today is our candlelight dinner time" I was thinking about this joke in my mind, this is my personal thing. Thinking about the worst can only make things worse, so why not just joke and relax.

Mom was finding the candles from the storeroom, and I was thinking about what we should do next to survive this storm. The windows were making sounds like they were cuddling roughly with air, and then there was Raining also to be part of this foreplay.

Things like these can actually break someone's trust in God or even in themself. It was not a normal rain and wind; they were like messengers of hell to send every one of us to heaven. The wind was blowing from left to right and my ears can feel it, that sound of the wind can make anyone mad but not my mother.

The woman who just a few minutes ago was terrified, is front of me smiling and told me to sit down piece fully and eat the rice.

How in the world can it make sense? She was in a totally different realm than she was before.

Maybe this is not about her, it's about me. Maybe she doesn't want me to get afraid, maybe she was pretending to be in control because of me.

We set down at our brown dining table and she serves me the omelet and brings more candles for us. The way she lightens up those candles is very peaceful and very hopeful. Watching her is like a Hope that this storm cannot kill me, or even can't damage me.

I was smiling while looking at her and she asked me

"what is it, Jeff? Why are you smiling son?"
I asked her "you are pretending! To be ok, why?" and her answer amazed me.
She said "no, not at all, why should I fear. I know God is with me, he was, he is, and he always will."
This simple line really blows up my mind because I can't believe how she can talk about god at this time, at this storm. The answer was very simple, GOD is her hope. A person can live without food and water but can never live without hope. If you think "I can live without hope" then this line you just read is hope in itself, "it is a hope of living without hope". Hope is our fuel, either good or bad. We cannot hope for bad that's why we think god is a positive power, think it that way that if the holy books suggest god is evil, the supreme power is evil no one will remain good, because everyone wants to be on the winning side, everyone wants their hopes to be met, that's why these books conclude that god is the light of positivity.

A normal person without any belief can be turned down and can be destroyed, but the one who believes in unseen power can never be destroyed on the mind level until he/she accepts that their hope is lost. That's why religious people are so bold in religious things because they think they are on the side of the most powerful being in the reality or even beyond it. GOD

As a science student, I can't believe in GOD in the sense most common people do. If God is real, then he cannot be "HE". We can address God as "IT". GOD is not a male or female but a power that creates the universe or we can say the universe is GOD. Either way "he" is not the way God should have addressed. But my mother can't understand this.

My Mom and I had fought before, but her confidence in GOD got me scared sometimes. It's not a bad thing to believe in God, but did she actually believe in GOD? or she is just drinking the seawater labeled as Rainwater

According to religious and holy books, we know what God wants from us, but how the hell anybody can know that what God wants from us or even if "it" wants something from us? Some say a profit of the Lord tells us and some say god takes form in humans, that's the bullshit thing I can't believe. God is GOD; if it creates the whole giant universe then it doesn't need any kind of profit for our little negligible earth and had not been born in form of humans.

GOD can be real, but these stories of God are not reality, some people reached huge success, but we cannot assign them as Gods or profits, and we should not too. If God wants something from us, he can just tell us, I don't think "It" doesn't speak.

But these all facts and logic came to an end after a simple line of religious people. “The one who doesn’t believe will suffer and the one who believes will get beautiful places in heaven”.

Fear and greed both are very much can seen by naked eyes there.

Questioning these holy books is marked as sins, but if God doesn’t want us to question, he would not give us the power to think logically.

While my mind is battling with itself, mom asked “why don’t you eat dinner? I made you your favorite combination of food” while smiling a little.

I came back to my senses. She was waiting for my answer that time and I am waiting for my mind to process and think of something sensible to say at this crucial moment.

“Mom, I really love you but can’t agree with you on this belief in God...I apologize”

She was silent for the moment but then she smiled and said “maybe you don’t have to apologize”

What the heaven I just heard, “Is this really my mother? Or otherwise, she was abducted by an alien race while on the way to the mosque” I was thinking about this genuine reason. After all she just said something this genuine to me.

She was still smiling and told me “sit down”

For 2 minutes I can only hear the voice of the rain showering on our window.

I listened to the woman who was just like my mother, she told me in her soft voice "God doesn't want you to believe in him, but want you to work according to him, work the right way. The people who killed your father think that they are impressing the mighty one, but in actuality, they are selfish and only think about themselves and this behavior will pay in the long run, they can justify themselves that they are on the road of heaven but their selfishness surely made a U-turn to hell. If you are doing selfishness in the name of religion or selfishness in the name of science and logic, either way, you are wrong and if you are doing something good, then it's good. As the old saying goes "the right is right, even if no one is doing it, wrong is wrong if even everybody is doing it"

After those lines, 2 things are for sure.

1. She was correct.
2. She is my mother and not an alien.

The 2nd one is far more relief maker than the first one, to be honest.

After this relief, we can finally concentrate on our dinner. I love the combination of rice, omelet, and potato chips. It's not healthy to eat rice at night; according to leading nutritionists having rice at night can increase your chances of being obese. But sometimes it's all about what we want not what we need.

After starting the dinner, the first 15 minutes are just silent and peaceful. After that, we finished it by talking a little about some normal household chats. She is regaining her smile but then suddenly there is a voice…….

The door opened because of the air pressure which was created by our beloved storm. The wind from outside took the fire and warmness of the candles with it and left the coldness and terror as rebates. The sudden moment of wind left us breathless on our spot, for a moment I thought it's not wind but the angel of death on our door.

My mother was in shock for a second. Then after some time, a cold breeze took place in her body and made her came back to her senses. "Jeff go and closes the door," she said while her eyes were in blinking mode like she was scared.

"And be careful also while closing it" she added her care.

While closing the door I heard voices from the sky, maybe the clouds are not happy with each other and there is a cold war placing right now. 'This is my mind and not me with these childish terms to describe the reality, but honestly, it's lovely to feel that the child most of us killed as in the name of maturity is still in me somewhere making these statements'.

After closing the door, I came back to my chair and sat on it. My eyes were on the non-flaming candles, so I blew them up with a matchbox, for some reason or another the voices from outside are stopped now. I can literally hear the crunchy sound of matchstick when producing fire. The silence is peaceful and watching the candles light up again is another kind of satisfaction for me.

My eyes were absorbing the light and warmth of that flame. It was like a flame of hope for me. Mother was looking at me and smiling. I caught her staring and asked "what??"

"Nothing Mr. Genius Just thinking about that you are too much innocent" She said.

"You really think I am innocent?" I said while thinking about the fun stuff I have done with my friends and girlfriend" I said with a little sarcastic smile.

"I am not talking about the girlfriend boyfriend stuff or friends fun dear, you thought I didn't know about it?" she said while looking straight into my eyes.

My smile was disappeared like I was watching my end in front of my eyes. I am a strict atheist, but desperate times demand desperate measure, so I prayed in my mind 'please the one above all, end this world right now and recreate everything as you please but just finish this conversation. Better is to make breaches from other dimensions and send some aliens who can kill me.'

"That's not the problem here," she said. Her words are like oxygen to my paralyzed brain and I came back to senses. "Innocence is not about what you do, but your intention while you do it" her words make sense to me.

I remember to do an important job. I switched to praying mode and cancel all the destruction shows I had just demanded.

"So, what is it then? How you concluded that I am innocent?" I asked to distract her as far as I can from the girlfriend's topic.

"Young man, you do things not to gain an advantage over others but to satisfied yourself without giving conscious trouble to others while doing it," she said this while made a cute loving sound we all make when talking to children.

'Mission accomplished. I successfully distracted her' I was thinking.

"See, you try to distract me without hurting my feeling, that's innocence," she said while her eyes sparkle, and a laugh came out from her mouth.

I joined the laughter with a fake smile, but in my mind, I lost my respect as a teenager who can't even hide his secrets from his mother. I broke my heart. All those dreams as a respected backbencher are shattered now.

“You looked like your father when faking laughter,” she said covering her mouth while laughing.
‘I hate myself, can’t even fake a laugh’ I became silent thinking this while making a puppy face.
“Don’t worry, your secret is safe with me young men, I am not going to tell your friends that I know mostly everything about your private life” she said these lines while placing her right hand on my left.
She actually can read me like a book. She knows that while her society is important for her, mine is important for me.
Fitting in society is important for almost every human. We can change our society, but we cannot live without one. Society of teenagers is very important for teenagers, as much an adult’s society is important for adults. Maybe on some level society of teenagers doesn’t make sense as an adult society but this also happens for the old man’s society, and this thing is called the generation gap.
We cannot say this or that society is good or bad. Society is just a union of people who agreed upon the same thoughts and these thoughts can change anytime. So, each and every society is of the same level and should be treated with the same respect also.
My mother knows this that’s why she respects this behavior that my teenage society taught me. It’s not about is it the right behavior or wrong, but about

respect towards a union thinking. I like this about her.
While thinking about all this conversation I thought that I can give her a welcome gesture. I took the utensils with me to the sink and started washing them, while I washed 2 of them, merry stopped me.
"Dear Jeff, no need of it. This evening is very cold, and I don't want my son to be in fever for the rest of the weekend." She said while taking a stand from the chair and coming towards me.
"Mom, you always told me to help you with the household work. Now if I am doing it then why stopping me?" I asked her this question sometimes, but she couldn't answer it.
"Oaky, but the answer is a bit tricky. You must understand it word by word. Promise me". She said while making uprising a pinky finger of her right hand.
This is our little, but serious game of pinky promise. Once we had a pinky swear then no matter what, we will not going to break it under any circumstances until that person with whom we had done the promise permits us to do so.
"Okay, I promise I will listen to it word by word of it". I said while uprising my pinky finger and then done the holy ritual of hugging pinky fingers with each other.

"I am going to tell you a secret about mankind and women kind also". She said while inviting me to sit over on the chair.

"I am listening". I replied after sitting on it.

"Man and women are not the same". She said while making big eyes.

"What?" I asked while being in the confusion about what I should get out of it.

"They are different, not only from bio-logical but also from a physiological perspective." She said while smiling and looking towards my nose. She moves her hand closer to it and pitches out dead skin from it.

"Okay, but in what ways and why you are telling me all this now?" I said while taking a looking at the dead skin she just took out from the surface of my nose.

"I am telling you all this because you asked me that, why I always told you to help me at home workings and when you finally do, I just stopped you," she said

"Fair enough," I said while nodding.

"Dear Jeff, you are living in a world which is actually full of surprises and sometimes common sense cannot answer the way it works," she said while blinking her big eyes several times.

"I can see this," I told her while thinking about how the universe sometimes doesn't play logic but only its own will. Black holes, supernovas, and moving galaxies are not common sense but to accept that the universe is different than what we thought it is like to be. The universe is sometimes far from easily digestible words and full of non-expected things.

"It's not only about the space wogi doogi Mr. Genius but about humans also," she said while smiling a little.

'Can witches be real?' I thought to myself. How the heaven she can read my mind like that?

"Humans are also different. Some wants hurdles, some wants heart, some wants hearing, and some wants solutions" she said while rolling her eyes and thinking about something.

"Didn't catch" I told her.

"Let's say you are having a bad day at school and it suddenly starts raining," she said this sentence by feeling the voice of rain on our terrace.

"Yeah, but why you send me to school in the rainy season. Not good one mother". She looks at me and after 5 seconds. We both shared a laugh.

"Oaky be serious now Mr. Genius," she said while taking a breath.

"I will become sad and think to take my mind off. Maybe I will arrange an umbrella and came back home"

"That's like a man. If you were in a problem, you will go and solve it." She said while smacking the table with a fast but not much powerful strike with her right hand.

"So, is there a problem with this attitude?" I asked her while thinking about what is her point?
"It's not about your attitude towards the problem but the attitude towards women who have the problem," she said while she takes a lean forward and then back again to relax her back.
"Did you mean the way we handle our problems is different than women handle their problems?" I questioned.
"Bull's-eye" she smiled like a kid.

THE DIFFERENCES OF DIFFERENT ONCE

The sound of the wind is now more terrifying and louder than the sound of rain. It can be taken under consideration that they were in a race to make the heart-attack process speed up. The direction of the wind got changed from right to left now, and my ears can again feel it. I got Goosebumps. So, to distract me from all this 'voice show' telecasting from sky or hell, I just paid more attention to my mother's voice. Her voice is high-pitched but very calm at the same time.

"Women don't want solution of the problem but rather a sympathy". She smiled a little, rolling her eyes to the ceiling while a small tear takes a room there on her eye.

"But how this can even make sense? Sympathy doesn't solve problems mother" I said.

"95 percent of time women don't need a solution but rather sympathy only. They want a rock to cry on and not a pebble that rolled over when got a little push". She said.

"But why mother? It's ill-logical to think or act like that". I said while being confused.

"Yes, it is ill-logical but emotional. We women are more emotional than logical". She stated this statement very proudly.

"This world governs by logic only mother mine. If emotions took the lead, then innovation will pay the price." I stated.

She took a deep breath and then said. "What is the main purpose for innovation or why you want to know the ultimate truth?" she asked.

I thought about it and then replied with a serious smile on my face. "Innovation is for the betterment of society, for the betterment of humans. And I want to know the ultimate truth about this universe or reality because I don't want to feel like an idiot who is just following nonsense tradition". I said while taking out my tongue for a second and take it back, in a funny manner.

"Yeah true," she said these words while making a sarcastic face.

I laughed a little in front of her and more inside my head.

"Can you see the irony in that little boy?" she asked.

"What irony?"

"You said it yourself that you don't want to feel like an idiot who is just following nonsense tradition," she said those words while giving an extra push to the "feel" word.

She continued "innovation is for the betterment of society. It is true, but how we came to the conclusion that we should innovate something new and good for our species? We came to this conclusion by a feeling called sympathy. Sympathy with other human beings and this sympathy is an emotion. So dear MR genius, you should think logically at the surface, but your core values should always be of good emotion. Get it?" she completed her statement, looked straight into my eyes while smiling and making dancing moves from her eyebrows.

"I think this information can help you in the long run of your life" and she winked at me like a girl's best friend. She was right.

I was literally speechless from her arguments because they were 100 percent to the fact.

I can't believe that the woman, who is so full of tradition, can be this much a fact person. She explains all this from a factual perspective to me, but then why she is too much scared to question those holy written quotes whose all focus is upon their tradition and not innovation.

"What is it young men?" she asked.

"Nothing" I covered. "If that's true that women just want sympathy and not any kind of solution then isn't this type of behavior will raise several problems in women's life?" I always asked a question like these and here also I continued my role.

She thought about it and then gives me a look. "I do think that that is true. We certainly do several things which are good for nothing. But we still do them because of our nature, because of our emotions. But you can't say to a lion to eat vegetarian food and to a cow to eat meat. It is what it is young man." She completed her saying and then took a stand from her seat to the kitchen sink.

I realized that while we are talking and I am listening to my Mother with every bit of concentration without considering other things in my mind, the wind and rain also do the same and took a break. Maybe this information is as new for them as it is for me.

I can hear the rough sound her feet are making while touching the tiles. The storming night is not too much stormy right now.

Normally teens of my age like loud music and adventure, and I am also of that type. But here right now, this silence is peaceful for me.

Maybe we all like this silence sometimes, or more precise if I may, then ... 'It is the silence that we need sometimes.'

LET'S BE CLEAR ABOUT TRUTH

The voice of water showering on utensils has stopped now. Mom was standing there in silence.

It feels like I have been sitting on that chair for a whole day. My bum feels senseless and when I leaped to get up from there, it felt like thousands of ants are crawling on it.

While controlling the crawling sensation I asked her "mother". She looked at me while making her wet hands waterless with a towel.

"How you can be that much logical and still follow this 'religion thing'? Don't you think once that this all is just a hoax? Every person definitely has questions about everything in the past when they were younger. But this 'religion thing' just shattered the human thing of exploring."

She was listening to all of this and her speed of blinking eyes can tell me that she was also in that "let me ask questions about beliefs to myself" state with herself.

After a deep breath, she responds "sometimes I feel it too Son. Our life can't be just about serving an unseen power. It had to be more than a mission to make some old power living 2000 floors above us happy."

She took the glass from the side and pour water into it. while she was filling the glass, I can hear that the wind is again on the run.
Maybe mother was sad because if she accepts this statement fully in her head, she must let go of all the hopes that these things gave to her. All the satisfaction she gets just by prayer.
'Did prayers do the real work? If a meteor hits the grounds and humanity gets a glimpse of what the universe can do with us? Prayers will not work if alien invaders make this planet a picnic spot for their fire range practice.' I was thinking.
"No, no. I can't think this way, it's a sin. God please forgave us. We should not disobey what you command us to do. We are humans who are here just for you on your beautiful planet." She continued the thinking of the person who is filled with fears.
I know that if I try to force my thinking on her this time then it would be catastrophic. It's a crucial moment so I told myself "just relax buddy, it's her thinking and you can only talk."
"Let me ask you a simple question" I sat on the chair again while muttering these words and folding my hands until they touch my chest.
She was still on her spot. Her eyes are filling with tears while she listens to my words and came to the reality from the uncertainty, she just experienced.

"Okay dear, go on" she allowed her mind for attention towards my question.
"Who is god?" I asked
After listening to this question, she took some time and came with an answer
"God is the creator of this world and father of all without a mother. He is there when the world has begun and he will be there when it will destroy. He creates everything and nothing can be done without his permission." She finished it all with one breath only.
"So without his permission, there will be no action" I clarified.
"Absolutely right, if he doesn't want it then no one can do it. That's why we are here alive and that's why we should thank him always."
A thunder strikes again. The voice is not that enormous but very surprising at the same time. I continued my childish but mature interrogation somehow.
"Oaky mother, let's stick to this point that without permission of God nothing can be done." She nodded after I finished this sentence. "But if this is true then why terrorists survive, why bribe still runs the system, women still have to suffer freedom issues and rapists still walk on the roads freely?"
She was in a bit of confusion after I ended my question. It's looked like that she is in

kindergarten's entrance exam and I handed her a question paper on quantum physics.

"Nice one, but these questions are asked before you and answered also in every religious way." She speaks after a pause in her voice.

Made a disgusted face for a second while massaging her left foot with her left hand and take the chair to be on my level.

"God gives us all an examination, in which we have to perform according to his commands and at the end of this, either we will get rewarded or punished. He is our teacher and a kind of supervisor." She said.

"But he is not our teacher, but rather creator. You said it yourself mother" I said.

"He is our all in one and always with us in every situation needed," she said.

"Everything means everything, the destroyer too?" I asked.

"Yeah, of course, he created everything, and he only has the right to destroy everything. Only he has the power." She said

"And destruction can happen in any way, right mom?"

"Yeah sure, it can be anything. A flinch, a flood or a bug that will end everything, but whatever it is gone be the wish of all-mighty one" She said.

"It means any kind of destruction can only be done by God himself?" I questioned.

"Yessss" her voice was a bit irritated and her eyebrows kissed each other a bit.

"Destruction of anything he created can only be done by him, either on my mind level or on a physical level"

"Yes son, sometimes destruction of mind can be brutal than physical, but every type of destruction or creation is done by him. Physical happenings are just outcomes of mental ones, anything mentally is done by god too. He gave us the power to control anger and he gave us the power to move on from the pain." she said while making herself calm again.

"That's the point. He is the only authority on destruction. Not the devil but the god is the only authority on this work." I said.

"Well, he only can destroy everything, from a bit to everything in the universe or the universe". She said.

"Then it means he is not good or power of positivity, the positive one can only do the positive work and not of destruction. Now please don't say something like sometimes destruction is better than other things. He is god so he can make a world that doesn't need destruction, that doesn't need death or any kind of pain." I said while making my eyes a little huge than usual.

"His world, his rules," she said this most annoying thing in a voice full of pride.

"So, is he a dictator?"

"How can you say that son?" she said while making her eyes wide.

"I am not saying it, you are saying it. His world his rules are the definition of a dictator" I said.

"Okay fine, but dictators are humans who pretend as a god, not a god who pretends as a god," she said.

"Yeah true, but we must accept that his wish was not that much perfect, if he creates humans then we should be perfect too. After all, we are created by someone perfect for the rest of eternity and reality" I said.

"It does make sense son, but we were perfect when we are in heaven, but the devil corrupts us. He corrupts us then and he lives inside each one of us now also," she said.

"Humans created by God, and devil corrupts us?" I asked.

"Yes son"

"But the devil himself also created by God himself, then who corrupted the devil? If I believe everything you say and everything mostly every religion offers us then it is the outcome at the end that the devil is the monster, but can't you guys think that this monster is created by the god himself too. Is that means he wants a monster or does he is not perfect in making things? Or is he a politician? But then the reasoning says, he doesn't need to be a politician if he can change our thinking and reality.

He created the devil as Devil and if the Devil is doing something devilish then it is not the fault of the devil that does destructive things but the fault of God who made him like that. After all, he is the overall authority on creation and destruction. He created him as he was or as he is. The Devil is the handmade monster made by God." I end it all like I represented a big thesis.

My mother was in shock after listening to all of this, maybe this time these sentences really turn the brain switch ON in her conscious.

Can this be the moment she can think out of the box?

All the big changes came from small moments like this. Some people think that all the great revolutions in the world come to existence by the relies upon or by people forming a big crowd but, in actuality, it all starts with some small change in one thinking, and who force or made every other person think like him\her.

I know that these religious things are not considered that much of a problem these days. But people who can see it that way can talk to their loved ones about it and hopefully can change their thinking.

In any case, either the person is logical or emotional, and if you try to convince him\her for something then you have to play by his rules.

My mother is logical, so I must present logic in front of her.

She was still in a mental shock and tries to think of something to get out of it.

"Son, the devil is bad, and God is good. How can you say that God created the devil as if he wants something bad? It doesn't make any sense."

"Dear mother, does any supernatural story ever made any sense? Some say that some God vomits this world into existence and some say that the earth is the center of the universe and sun and moon and all the stars revolve around them."

"But son ours is different. Our religions contain many scientific facts and many of them have proofs too." She said.

"Of course, Mother mine. Every religion has some good in it and very little bad if we see closely, most of them want to end one social evil or another but in doing so they gave birth to another one"

I am not shouting but my words are clearly winning the voice competition against the sound of wind roving on the windows.

"Mom, if you created something like a machine and you are perfect at creating them and it turns out to be a bad machine then it is not the fault of the machine but yours only. If God made devil, then only, he, The GOD should be addressed and blamed for every bad thing devil had done till the moment" I stated.

"Son, it's not fair at all. If I raise you with morals and ethics but you turn out to be a bad person then it is not my fault but yours. You can make your own decision."

"Mother, I can only become that type of a person if my surroundings are of that type, but when God created the angels there were no surroundings, it was just nothing according to the old sayings. And parents have no power over a child's learning ability as does God have. He can create a good angel without any agony or jealousy in it, but he chooses not to. Ask yourself why?"

There was a shock on her face now; it's like a lot of thunder strikes there too.

"I don't know why? It could be a big plan of him" she said.

"What big plan mom?"

"Maybe to give people an example of good and bad, an example of what they are allowed to do or what they are not allowed to do. Maybe they want to give us a sign so that we can be better kids than he had before"

"Dear mother, don't you think that making your son do evil or make him evil just to set an example for other children is a bad thing to do?"

I continued. "And maybe we are actually not allowed to destroy this earth that's why we don't have that kind of power. And if he really wants to give us some signs then why not gave us directly, just like gravity, or just say it with clear words in their respective languages. I don't think he can't speak or don't know the latest trend in the languages"

My words are like M416 of PUBG for her (it's a gun in the mobile game, and frankly it's my favorite one.)

"Son, what you are saying does make sense, but can't you understand that this religion thing gives us hope and a sense of doing something good also. We are humans and we cannot always be right if we take delicious based on our emotions. We need a discipline that should be the center of our lives and it should be the basis of ethics but every human will be going to change it under one situation or another until unless this or any other religion put him under a brain pressure to not do the things emotions demands but to do the work, discipline craves" her words are clear like her forehead skin without any curvy lines on it, it means that she is not having any kind of stress but total thinking only.

This time she got an AWM I guess.

"and son" she continued in her calm but authorized voice "I know you think that religion is fake, but it is not a fact like gravity but just your perspective, every person has his own perspective and according to that he decides what is true for him and according to him." she took a pause.

And concluded, "For us, reality and truth are just what we think of them in our mind" she took a break to breathe.

"Son, I know you angry at these traditions where other people told you what to do but son you have to accept that many times in life people need hope more than they need food. There has to be a perspective which supports this thing all along, otherwise what people will count on?"

"mother, I totally get your point but why don't just tell them the truth that there is nothing like religion or what they think is the way of god is just another way of some human who thought that this was a better way to live life 1800 years ago. People should know the reality and not just get to know the perspective. I know you think this is just my perspective, but just think about it once" I said.

"Okay, let's do it your way son. Let's assume that if these traditions are not in existence, then what do you think? What will happen to this world and our humanity?" she asked.

"Let's say that this world will be at a very good place than it is at today, no more blackmailing on the stuff of reincarnation or telling people what will be going to happen in hell if they don't do this or that. This world will be not based on some stupid caste system and people can be with the person they actually love and not with them who are suitable for their family name or so-called bull shit"

"I get it son, but do you think these will be the only things that will change. You got some positive thinking there, now let me show you some negative sides now. The fundamentals will remain the same, the people who used god and his holy books as a guide to take advantage of others will find another way to do so, they will again start to manipulate the innocent once with other things. People may be not blackmailing other people based on hell or heaven but sure they were doing the same job with some heavy weapons. In the times of old ancient rituals, the law was not an option as it is today. That's why there had to be an authority which would be able to control them."

I really don't want to be on the religious side, but she was right on this one.

"Oaky son, so do you think that you hate all old traditions made by religions?" she asked.

"Yeah, sure I do".

"Okay, then do you think that doing something good for others without showoff is a bad thing?" she questioned.

"Of course, not mother, it is a wonderful thing to do, because we should be doing good things because they are good things and not to gain sympathy or attraction or some kind of attention," I said.

"That's correct. Most religions told us to do this kind of goodness without any kind of showoff, in fact in holy books it's written also that you should not say your good works out loud because it means that you have done that thing to show that you are a

good person, not because you really are one." Mother said.
"But then why this points system is there, if you do good things then you will end up in heaven and if don't then you have to settle for hell. This is just a manipulation to make people do what religion decides to be as good work" I said. *
"But son, religion does describe all the good things that we should do. But the entire things humans do are because of some motives, so here making god happy is a motive or angry is a motive to do or not do some specific things" She said.
Yeah, it is true, and I accept that this really helps some humans. Frankly, she is right, all the people in this world do something because of some motive or inspiration, if there is none to drive them then no one can do or even want to do anything.
"Oaky mother, what you said was right, but it is not about how they did it only but also about how they get to choose everything for us. No one has the right to designate a life for someone else, no one in this world like to be controlled without their will and these people who wrote religion books or people who said they are the messenger of God are doing this with us, maybe some of them are thinking for the sake of us, but even though they have no right to abandon us for loving a person who is not of our clan, no one has the right to write our destiny to serve an unseen power without even asking from us,

no one has the power to make us feel that we are not good enough if we don't do things In a specific manner" I stated.

"So, then what do you want son, that people on this planet should do wars or take wrong paths in the name of freedom?"

"No mother, it is not what I wanted to say, people never fight in the name of freedom as much as they do in the name of religion by the way. But there are not only two ways to live a life, not just religious or being a person who should be put behind bars. Just like there are not only two occupations to pursue but millions of, it is the same way there are not only two roads to walk on but many many more".

Mom took a sip of water from the glass.

"Okay, gentleman. So, what do you think a better world could be like? Because if you really think you should end this religion thing then you must give humanity something in return. So, what is that you give it back?"

I really don't expect that she will question me about how this world should look like in terms of betterment, but now she did. So, just take a look at a world where morals don't need a train of religion to reach a station of happiness and fulfillment.

let's take a look towards that world.

WINDOW TOWARDS A NEW WORLD

A world where there is no religion but just moral education on its behalf. Where people don't serve an unseen god but serve everyone's true needs of growth and happiness.

While waiting for my answer, mom keeps blinking her eyes and I am still thinking of a world that will be perfect according to my perspective.

"If religion vanished from this world but all the values of individual's privacy still remain somehow then this world will be a place where wars cannot be done in the name of religion at least"

"Pardon please," she asked to explain in detail.

"The people who pick up weapons in the name religion are actually get manipulated by other people who wants profit from fear and wars. The people who called as terrorists did wrong things while thinking that they are doing the utmost right things for their community and for their god" I said.

My words are the only sound my mother and I can hear, all the other voices that came before from outside have now vanished.

I took a sip of water and hear the sound of it going down to my stomach from my throat.

“Anything else mister?” she asked.

“There is more than enough wondering about that kind of world mother mine”

It’s true; a world without even a single thing can make a huge difference to the outcomes of reality we can imagine but a world without religion is a thing I am very happy to put a thought on. It can be a world with my father in it, where some mentally unstable people will not kill him to save their conscious thinking.

If a murderer gets a death sentence because of his\her action of killing a person, then the people who killed my father should get a worse punishment than a death sentence, all these people thought they can do these types of things because they are on the path of their gods, but the people who kill other people because of their religion issues are no less than the terrorists who gets hated globally.

And it's not just about doing wrong but who have the intension also, many people in the world can't kill someone but they have pure intentions of it.

As my mentor **Z** once said, "if people believe in God and pray for someone's death, then it is an attempt to murder."

Mother was on her chair and I was thinking about the world without caste problems and where there are no discriminations.

"What are you thinking son?" she asked.

"Mother, I was thinking that in the world like that people will not get categorized based on caste and religion. They have the right to be whatever they want to be, being with whoever they want to be without any emotional pressure" I said.

"Son, this is not fair. In today's world too we can be with anyone we want or be anyone we want. We have the law on our side for this" she said.

"Yes mother, the law is on our side, but we are emotional creatures and most of the people get blackmailed by stupid emotional acting. Some people even think that if their children do something beyond religion or caste's limits kinds of stuff then it is the end of their own life. They think people around them think less of them but all the people around them or around us are now know that they also have their own problems, so no one is interfering with other's privacy until unless the person who is interfering have a selfish goal of his\her own, like thinking that by stop people to flourish their actual love they are doing a favor to god but they can never be more wrong" I said.

"Son, how can you say it is selfish? If they are doing that for god" she asked.

"Mother, the people who have the intension to kill or to stop someone who done something beyond caste or community's or religion's limits are actually thinking that they are doing some favor for god but they are only making selfish choices for themselves according to their own beliefs, they are no less than murderers," I said.

I stood up from the chair because of the pain in the left rib that I got by sitting on the chair for so long.

I looked at the watch and the clock show 2:25.

She was still on her chair waiting for me to elaborate on the reason to her; maybe she also wants to know the reason she had to raise her child all alone.

"Mother, the most important reason some people stop others is just to remain in power, let me pardon. Most of the people think that 'if my daughter or son get to indulge in business other than my social group allowed then their life will be tough and no one will be there to help my children', and some other people took advantage of this week state of their mind by giving them the solution that they are with them, but in reality, they are just there to show some kind of power and gain control over others for their own benefits" I said.

"Yes son, I agree on this that people really took advantage of other people. I agree that people who killed your father are in no way threatened by relationship of ours in any way and they choose to end a life just in the name of religion, but this doesn't mean religion is a bad thing. It's just like you are upset because of a knife somebody used to cut his wrist. But you can't blame that knife, it is just a tool. You cannot blame the knife just because someone is using it in a wrong way" She said.

"You are right mother, on each and everything you just said, and yes blaming the knife will be the bad thing to do, but who in the heavens gave that knife to someone who doesn't even know its real use?" I said.

"What do you mean by that?" she asked.

"Mother you are right about the theory that religion is just a tool, but just like the person who cut off his wrist, most people are doing wrong with themselves and with their loved ones in the name of religion. We don't give the knife to kids because we know they can't use them correctly and end up hurting themselves" I said.

"Are you saying that we as humans are not developed to be religious?" she asked

"I am saying that almost all people who follow religions don't know why religions are made in the first place," I said.

"Son, maybe you were right about it. Maybe we all really don't know how or who made these religions. Maybe it is a god who sends books and angels to us or people who made them according to that time's need but then how can you say, that you know the reason why they came into existence" She said.

"NO, I don't know for sure. I only can observe and understand, ask questions, and then came to some answers, that's how all the big discoveries came into existence, by thought processing. But I accept the fact that we don't know everything about the reality we live in" I said.

"Okay, go on" she allowed my words.

"There are always some minor differences between each and every religion, but let's jump to some big similarities that all these religions have in common," I said.

"What Similarities? The only similarities of religions are believed in God (the supreme power) and do good things in the name of him. What else there could be?" she asked.

It's wired that this time her expressions are telling me that she doesn't have any idea of this similarity thing.

Maybe people ignore what they have in front of them the most.

"There are many things mother." I smiled.

"One of the most common things in any religion is an after-course reward" I continued.

"What?" her face was like a meme I saw on the net today.

"All religion promises to deliver an afterlife reward in the name of heaven or places where you will go after death. This is the most appealing thing religion can offer, they promise to deliver a place where everything is perfect, where you will get the things, you want the most, but that is the flaw here. Nothing in the whole universe can complete a human's greed of 'want'" I said.

“the reality is people get satisfied in one way or another. Some monks are happy without anything on mountains, rich people who are smiling in their big mansions, and middle-class people who have the same smile as those others in their small house. In reality, it is not about wants but needs, they all are happy because they concentrate on what they need and they already have what they need to be happy, but most religions make our greed of wants a weapon to control us. That is the difference here” I said.

“So, you think that religion uses our greed as a weapon?” she asked.

“That’s the point. Do you ever ask yourself that why most of the things that are forbidden for you in this world are delivered as a reward in the afterworld?” I said.

“Maybe this is his grand plan,” She said.

I really love this improvement when she used the word “maybe” in her statement; it means that she can accept that there can be more ways than only once being told.

“Mother, if treating women as their slaves is a sin here then it cannot be a privilege there, if living inside some home and not doing anything is not ideal here then it cannot be an idea of the piece there, if more of anything is the problem here then there is no way it can be a blessing there," I said.

I can tell from her face that she doesn't love my idea that much.

"Son, why are you comparing the cosmic world with the social one? Don't you think maybe it is a bit narrow-minded thinking?" she asked.

I really don't see that coming from her. If a religious person talks about not having an open mind, then you must understand that you are hitting some spots there.

"Mother, from the very begging all of the religions in the world there is a comparison of all mighty with a father figure. Don't you think it is the biggest comparison of the cosmic world and the social world?" I stated.

Her eyes make a gesture this time, and while going to the left and then right side; it sends a signal that she understood what I was trying to convey her.

"It is true, and I have to accept the truth here. But I am not accepting anything else, young priest." She said while her words contain pride and a little anger in it.

"Of course, mother mine, I never want to make you feel pressured. I just want to tell you what I think of this world and just want you to think about the possibilities out there of the reality and the truth." I said.

"All right, what are the other similarities?" she asked.

"All religion needs a savior and an enemy," I said.

"I don't think so that religion needs a savior, after all a thing god made for us doesn't need to be saved. And what enemy are you talking about other than the devil?" she asked.

"Mother each and every religion shows us a savior in their history, either it can be their profit, either it can be god himself in some form or another, or relative of god are also present. No matter what the religion, there was someone who came to existence as the savior of that religion." I said.

"But those types of saviors, profits, and forms of god are needed to tell people what is right and wrong, to tell what their or our religion is all about. Those saviors are needed for betterment" She said.

"Maybe they are needed for the betterment, but the betterment of what mother? Is it humanity that needs betterment or religion that demands it?" I asked.

"What difference does it make if either of those needs it?"

"A Huge one, according to almost every religion, they had a concept of begging of the world, if it true then nature and religion were on the same level. They both are equally powerful because they both are present at the very beginning; they both are starting steps of everything but then why religion needs saviors and on the other hand, nature doesn't need any" I said.

"What do you mean by that? Religion needs a savior because people don't have that much sense to understand it. God sends his precious just to clarify things, and according to some other religion, he took forms also to do the same task."

"Mother can't you guys just thought for once that according to your own theory he is the almighty, if he really wants to do something then he will do it in a flinch. Nothing needed to do what he desires other than his own desire" I said.

"Maybe he wants us to take a lesson from it and without a story, we can't grasp the knowledge he wants us to understand, it's his way," She said.

"Okay, but you said that he wants all the people in the world to live in harmony and peace," I said.

"Yes, we are his children, and any person who once became a parent knows this that he\she doesn't want their children to fight with each other in any situation," She said.

"Mother then why not he just ends our thinking of 'fighting'? You said that he always wants to protect the good once, then why doesn't he make everybody good and genuine? You said he doesn't want his children to fight with each other, so why not he just ends these Wars, after all, he is the supreme power." I asked.

"In religious terms and according to my study, god made heaven and hell, and both need fuels to run and souls of good people are the fuel of heaven and bad once belongs to hell. If everybody will become good then no one will remain good, it will become common, not genuine" She said.

"That's the one," I said.

"Mother mine, according to religious beliefs heaven and hell are places where people spend their afterlife, but why there are only two of those kinds and not infinite like; a place for musicians, a place for technicians or a place for atheists?" I asked.

"Son, atheists are people who don't believe in god and according to the religious people sayings, the atheist will be going to burn in hell and that's the reason I was afraid that you will get a bad afterlife just because of your beliefs," She said.

"Mother, you my dearest well-wisher and this type of caring behavior is fully expected from you, you don't want me to be in any kind of trouble and that's why if there will be the single and slightest possibility of a problem for me according to your belief system then you will be going to stop me from walking onto that path," I said in the most genuine manly voice I can come up with at that time of night because frankly, I was about to yawn.

It was 3 AM on the clock.

The storm was still on the run, I guess because the wind is still on the roar but due to the door and windows, they cannot take full possession of our brain's terror part.

"But mother" I continued. "A world without religion will be a world without heaven and hell, people will not be going to impress the all-mighty by doing some old rituals which are not useful in the new time era. That world will be free of terror produced by hell and greed produced by heaven; it will be a world full of morals only where everybody has rights and doing good work is appreciated because it is good only, and not because of anything else. A place where people start to care for those who are around them because of the emotions and not just because God says so in some book." I stopped.

She was in silence for a bit and I was sitting there just feeling this awkward silence between us, and then she said.

"Son, what are you saying can be true but what if it is a necessity for the world around us?"

I was a bit confused.

"Let's think what could go wrong if religion was not been born?" she said.

MOTHER'S PERSPECTIVE

The rain has started again; water drops on the roof are playing knock-knock games with us but this time with 4x speed.

"Son, every religion was first started just to enhance mankind in a direction of goodness and away from one social evil or another. If we closely study the religions then we will know that every religion was established when there is actually a need of it, some religion wants to save the money while others want to save some animals, some wants to respect the elders while others want the protection of the young once, some wants women to be saved from slavery and some wants a decorate way to lead a family or a clan. All these religions are like laws without police or government; they are there to keep the bad within us in the name of god or his fear. Just think once that many of the old traditions are now part of our daily life like brushing our teeth, eating 3 or 4 times a day, bathing, making homes, find jobs for survival and for social approval, put on clothes and many more. These all things are not necessary as humans because we are not born with them but these traditions are now part of us due to continues practice and we cannot say that all of these are right but we can say that we cannot live without them now. But if all the social evil I mentioned became our part of daily life, then we cannot escape that mentality also and that's why all of these religions had to be there that time because that was not just the establishment of religion but also a revolution against some social evils" She said.

I was stunned at that time; she was like a great speaker we generally listen at ted talks.

"You are right mother, but isn't it bad that they don't tell us the truth?"

"If your theory is right and people back then created religions just to stop some social evils, then it is just like stopping a child going to the kitchen by saying there is a bogyman there, not to scare her from dark places for the rest of her life but to save her from fire and oil that might slip on her\him," she said.

"Alright mother, are you saying we are not ready for the truth back there as humans?" I asked.

"If what you said is true then yes, maybe laws and science are presented to us in the form of religion, just because we are not ready for the study of it. After all, we all need a reason to live and live with some mission, we all are doing this back then and we all are doing this now too."

Her voice was calm and truthful; there was no terror in it and not either greed.

We live in a world where we all want to feel something special, something beyond that can be a reality for all of us to achieve, something that can be socially approved and accepted, but the truth on the other hand is very rare to be accepted by society, not because we don't need to but because we don't want to.

"Son, even if you are right about all of this, it doesn't make any change in the past," She said.

"But mother it will truthfully change the future, maybe that child doesn't know how to enter into the kitchen but people who are well educated and understand logic can now take care of themselves. That kid is all grown up now. It is time to stop scared from bogie man's stories and explore the world as our true human nature demands it from us, with curiosity and ambition, without traditional boundaries and without thinking that our steps, 'those are not harmful to innocent people will going to make god unhappy'. We should live in a world full of morals and ethics and not of greed and fear."

After finishing the sentence, I just sat there with a little silence.

Mother was looking downwards with her lips open a bit and her forehead with a small wrinkle on it.

"What happened, mother?" I asked.

"Nothing much, it's just...." she paused and continued to stare at an invisible doormat, I guess.

"It's just?" I asked.

Mother said, "As a mother, I can think upon your logic but as a child of God I cannot accept these things, how do you feel if somebody would tell you

that I am not your mother or you just happened out of nowhere?"
"A great author once said- everything which exists is capable of its proof".
She was confused like she was thinking that, what she should take out of this.
"Son, god sends books and profits just to give us signs. He just doesn't want us to see him"
I was really thinking about what I should say. Should I say something to interrupt her believes or should I say something that is right according to me? Or should I remain quiet to let her understand what this nature teaches her?
No matter what relationship name we have, it begins with a need to be loved without condition and acceptance without change, we all should love without making boundaries in our head for our loved once and if someone we loved has different believes than us then we should accept that and just play along the game called life, this is the best way to enjoy the life.
But what we are doing here is not enjoying but exploring our beliefs and finding what is hidden in words that were spoken a long time ago. Many times, this does bring kayos between the mindsets we have.
"Mother" I start the conversation again after some seconds "if God really wants us to act according to a guide or a path which was introduced 10000 years

ago then we can't do anything other than that particular one, after all, he is the ultimate power with control over every dam thing," I said.

"Son, I am just a normal person with average knowledge of religion. Why don't you ask these things to people who are actually capable to answer your question?" she asked.

"I know what you want to say here, you still think that you are the one who lacks the knowledge to answer my questions, this is the problem here that we think 'we are the problem' and no the past situations. Religion made us believe that it is perfect, and we are the ones making mistakes, but don't you guys can see with your eyes that nothing in this whole universe is ever perfect. A child born or an elder who died was not perfect in every form or the sun that has black spots or the stars that get collapsed as black holes. This universe or what we can call nature never represents something as perfect but just better. Better understanding, better animals, better body, better health or better energy but nothing is perfect in this world. But we all humans believe that religion is perfect even if there are thousands of logical loopholes in it, we don't want to believe that it contains problems. Not because we think it doesn't, it is because we are too much comfortable with what we believe that we neglect what truly it is." I finished my words.

Her eyes are filled with fear and tears.

Maybe she was sad because she was failed as a mother to make her son believe in the one thing that gave her hope to live life: her beliefs in God. Maybe she was feeling guilty because she cannot take up the tradition of religion to her son as her ancestors have done in the past.

If I was brought up in the same environment with the same people and the same education, then there will be no difference in the thinking pattern of both of us.

She was right in her place, we humans are habitual creatures and do things that are comfortable, these all traditions she follows from the very begging of her life are felt safe for her.

I am challenging her hope and habits at the same time and she has all the rights in the world to feel bad about it.

"Son" her voice finally came from her vocal cord as a relief after the silent storm. "May I ask you a question?" she said while making an extra push on the "YOU" word.

"Of course, mother mine, anything you want" I answered.

"How you can be sure there is the sun in the sky? Or how you can be sure that what is the observable size of the universe? What makes you think that what these scientists publish in their papers are actually valid hypotheses and not just perspective mistakes of the human mind?" she asked.

‘This is not just one question, I was thinking. But this is not the right time to take that as a defence.
I can see what my mother is doing. Sometimes the best defence is an offense. When we target someone’s belief system, they generally attack ours just to feel safe. It is the same as when our parents told us to study for board exams and we ask them about their grades at the time when they pass out, (until unless your parents are toppers, if that’s the scenario then I have a deep feeling of sympathy for you guys.)
“Mother, breaking religious rules made us sinners, and breaking physics or chemistry laws make us Nobel Prize winners,” I said.
“This is not the answer to my question,” she said.
I can sense the seriousness in her tone. Now is not the best time to make some jokes in my head.
“Mother I know all these things from careful observation and research. All the data that has been collected till now are been collected by machines. And it can’t be a perspective mistake of the human race” I said.
“How can you be sure about it?” she asked while making an angry-looking face “what makes you think that religious statements are hoax presented as facts and statement of science on the other hand is genuinely trustworthy? After all, these are just statements” she asked.

Her words are true, I hate many things about old traditions but what I most hate about them is that most of the old traditions and religion "don't teach us how to think but rather what to think". If science would have done the same then there is no way back off from a future that is darker than the black hole.

But it is not what it looks like, science never told us what to think but told us how to think and then we find our answers.

"Mother, did you mean that as religion and science told us same things the same way?" I asked.

"Not in every aspect but in some maybe, science just announces that the universe is expanding and you believed it, science just said about those physics laws and you accept them. Why? You are also just accepting the statements as it is represented towards you by these people known as scientists" she asked.

It is a bit funny for me; she was asking questions like science is a group of people believing in a way to see the world. I must end this confusion by now.

"Mother, science is not like a clan who believed in a single statement, they are not people who lived with each other by following some kind of rituals. 'People who want to know how this world really works are scientists. These people are not born from a particular clan, they can be anyone, they can be from anywhere, science is not a study that can only be studied by people who are born in a particular religion, city, country or even on a particular planet. The only thing you should have to study science is curiosity to pursuit. the most beautiful thing about science is that it produces the same results in the same situation and be consistent about it."

She was looking at me with that angry bird look on her face again.

"I know madam, that is not the answer to your question," I said these words in a hope that she will spare my life for the greater good, and the best thing is she did.

THE IMPORTANT UN-SMILARITES

"The reason why most of the wise people and giants of this earth believe in science is that, that it represents data based on research and unbiased information. Every discovery science made till date was submitted as a fact and also as an answer sheet to common people and other scientists too. Anyone who found mistakes in it and corrects it will be going to get a price for it, like fame, prestige, job and sometimes even a great amount of money too."
She cut me off in the midway by saying ". really? they give money if somebody corrects it?"
"yes, mother mine, a real scientist has no shame in making mistakes because they know thats how it works. They will be going to do thousands of mistakes to able to get to know that one equation or info that they have been searching for years, and in some cases 'for decades" I said.
She was listening to all of this like a 10 years old girl who has been told that there are 100 more shades of colour in lipsticks.
"There are 2 most amazing and un similar things about religion and science. First is the way they proceed; one way where science introduced new and better ways to everything, religion just made us

believe that the only right and truthful ways were created in the past."

She stopped me and asked, "what is that supposed to means?"

"Listen to me closely, while great mind's extraordinary efforts of last century gave us some mind-blowing techs, we have to accept that now these techs are just a chapter in some school books. We are developing very fast, what once was a trial error success of 10000 times is now work of just a mechanic, and I am sure that what was 'next to impossible' in this century will going to be a child's play in the next one"

"what was your point?" she asked.

"my point is, that while science is all one way of developing things, religion made us believe that the only good or best things had already been happened. All great profits are already gone, all great magics of god have already happened and there is nothing better left to us for the future, there cannot be a better profit than the previous one, there cannot be better humans than the previous one, there cannot be a better world than the previous one. Religion taught us we are sinners but not that we can develop more with our curiosity. They told us that the best was left behind and we must follow that past to be good, but science told us that the greatest is yet to come and we have to keep exploring to find them." I ended my whole para with a spark in my eyes because honestly, I also don't know how I can say those points in just some fraction of minutes.

"well, it is true that religion said that there will be no other son of god, no other favourite profit of the lord, no other god will take form in the human body but..." she stopped.

"but what mother?"

"There are some people who claimed as the messengers of god now and then, what about those people," she said.

"hahahahha" a burst of laughter came out of my mouth.

"mother, do you really think that they are genuinely the messengers of god or even honest human beings?"

She was hesitated "Not all".

"not all? (sarcastic tone) not even a single one of them" I said.

"But son, some show magic that they have learned from the all-mighty"

"oh please, don't even get me started on that thing mother" my voice and face were filled with disgust but then I remember that we just had a fight some hours ago and I don't want to feel a déjà vu at this hour of the night.

I calm myself down a bit.

"mother, not even a single one of them is authentic out there," I said.

“But what about people who produce gold from hands, or people who read minds with just a glance,” she asked.

“you remember the magician I showed you on the tv last Friday, the magician walked on water, take credit card numbers, predict the future, and many more too. They are human too, but at least they show us that they are a trickster. These self-claimed gods are no more than average kind mentality humans who just learned a few tricks”

She was not upset by this statement because deep down she also knows about this reality.

I continued with “mother, just think about it that if they can really do this kind of magic by the grace of God then why not the person who takes out gold from thin air help all the poor people in the world? Why not the person who can read people's minds take a look at terrorist’s pic and spoke out his/her plan to save millions of lives? Why the person who can predict the future don’t tell him all followers the answer to the questions they will get in their child’s exams or interviews?” she was quiet while I was questioning her.

“Maybe this kind of power can only be used in some essence only” her voice was sounded like a confused kid who doesn’t the difference between the hour’s hand and the minute’s hand of a clock.

“Mother if they are special then they should be special all the time, the magicians are just doing tricks that's why they have a limited area in which they can perform and it is the same for these self-claimed gurus"

The speed of the wind is very slow right now and I can hear the bird's chattering.

"it's morning," I said, sometimes time really passes by quickly if what we are doing is intrusting for us.

After a few moments, she asked "what is the 2nd one?".

"what?" I don't understand her question.

"you said there were 2 dis-similarities between science and religion, then tell me the 2nd one" she demanded.

"Oh yes, the 2nd beautiful thing and one of the most powerful differences between religion and science is that 'evidence made the results in science but in religion, the results made the evidence'" she doesn't understand my thinking and asked for clarification in a non-verbal way by her hands.

"Mother, applications of science like gravity or motion are constant and produce same results in same conditions but on the other hand mantras of religion and lines from sacred religion never produce same results, in fact, if something good happens people will say 'god made things better and if something horrible happened then they will say 'it could have been worse, what God had done is better than that anyway', means no matter what the road those people walk through they will always already know the answer, or better if I elaborate then 'they only think that they know the answer'."

The sound of birds chattering was louder than before and sweeter too.

I continued to talk while she continued to listen "What I am trying to say is this that science wants to find how this universe works by exploring, no matter how crazy the results are. And religion wants to give us an already decided outcome by obtaining any road, no matter how crazy they are. That is the problem, in the first one we are finding what is our reality, and in the second one we are looking for ways that fit in our reality." I ended both my statement with a smile and cross my arms like an 80s hero.

Mother was there listening to all of this and focused on each and every single word of mine, she was processing all the information I just threw at her, and then she came up with the answer.

"Jeff, everything you just said made pure sense to anyone and it does make sense to me too but I don't understand one thing"

"what is it, mother?"

"Do you ever think, what is the real problem?" her face was glowing in spite of that she did not sleep last night at all.

We were talking all night about this and that, and now there is no night at all, the day was about to get started and the wind was at its natural pace.

Maybe the storm was long gone now and the only scenario I have to deal with is my mother's question.

THE REAL PROBLEM

"What do you mean by the real problem? The real problem is traditions and religious values that take core possession in the deepest corner of human minds" I said.

"Are you sure?" she asked.

"of course, just think about it, people back then who had a different belief system than their surroundings, are represented as monsters. We all are wired by some old thought processing to not accept change as a natural process itself. We have to change this thinking otherwise nothing will be going to change for the greater good."

"But son, again I will ask you the same question. What is the real problem?" she said.

I cannot understand why she was asking this same question again and again.

"I don't understand what do you mean by this question?" I asked.

She smiled a little and said "you said yourself that science is all about exploring and finding what is this world is actually like and you want to take that road. So, first, you have to find the real problem because of which this all is happening, and if you think that the problem is the belief system of people

then you have to ask why people have that kinds of believes"
She was right. As my mentor, Z once said "if you want to finish a problem you must seek its deepest root like you are standing on treasure box which is deep underground beneath you, so you have to get a spade and power to dig until you reach to the treasure, here TREASURE is the root cause of your problem, 'POWER TO DIG' is your BRAIN and 'SPADE' is the word 'WHY'"
On the surface, the traditional belief system is the problem and that's why we are following a path blindly. But I have to put my spade here and ask the deeper question, why we have this belief system? how we get to this point, of believing in supernatural entities and not pursuing logic as our true Human nature demands.
If we thought about it, we can see that people are not always like that, nature build us with a sense of sympathy and self-centeredness, that's why you will see that little babies want to help everybody in a need but at the same time are really selfish too for their own survival, they will not care if their mother is sleeping, they will be going to wake her up if they were hungry.
The reason why they are self-centered and nice to everybody and help at the same time is simply that that's what a real human being should be like, that's what nature made us into.

So, how and why we became a ruthless, blind, and divided killing machine today as human beings? Who is making their own kind bleed in the name of something that may or may not happened 10000 years ago?

If I ask, why we became what we became today then I can't have the absolute answer, because I don't know the exact unwritten reason of ancient history, but we can ask why this behaviour is continued till this date.

Why people still obey the unseen lie and neglect the clear truth? And the answer to this 'why' lies inside the survival phycology of human beings.

We are doing this because people around us are doing that, and they are doing it because we are doing it. This is the real problem; it is a chain reaction.

From the evolutionary perspective, our mind is there to save us, and from the very begging of human history we are always safer when we are in groups and not as individuals, we are safe from predators as a group and much powerful in case of natural calamities.

Just like the old story where a bundle of sticks is more powerful together than individuals, we are more powerful together than we are alone. Our mind learns this trick and used till this time but not in the same manner we thought it would.

Frankly speaking, our mind is a big selfish fearing baby and it does whatever it has to do to keep itself safe, and by itself, I mean us too.

Now our brain is too much attached to this behaviour that we don't want to offend the group as a whole and can lose our safe place.

We are creatures of emotions and that's why we are more attached to the feeling of being safe rather than being in a safe situation; like we are always surrounded by meteors, planets, black holes, and stars that can easily wipe us out from existence but we felt safe inside our home, why? Not because it is safe but because it is habitual, comfortable, and gave us a feeling of safeness.

"it is a chain reaction mother; we are doing this kind of behaviour because others around us are doing that, and others are doing this because we are doing it. We are influencing others and others are doing the same to us. we are in a chain where we are the matches and fire as well" I said.

"So, how can you end this chain reaction?" she asked.

I stood up from the chair and walked towards the window, the Sun was about to rise.

"The only way to end this is to step back and end this chain and let the actual nature of our existence take over as it should be," I said.

"And how can you do it? What if you stepped back and someone else took your place in that chain? After all, there are lots of people around" she said.
"of course, mother mine, there are millions even billions of people in this chain but we have to do what should be done in a peaceful manner and not in a fear transmitting sensation, the honest way to make people think about them is to give them knowledge, tell them how it can benefit them in the long run and just let them decide what they actually want to do, without any pressure. This is the only way they can be stick to it" I said.
"But son, people in religious values are also very disciplined and they are also choosing what is right for them," she said.
"mother, it is true that they are disciplined but they are always under the pressure of an unseen entity who is keeping records of good and bad works. They are just doing what is kind because they fear, not because they love or adore, and once the fear is gone there will be just negative chaos" I said.
Mother was about to say something but I stopped her and continues.
"I know mother, I am not someone who can predict the future but this is human nature, we need a continuous force for doing something but that force should not have the core value of fear or greed," I said.

"Yeah, you already told me about that son," she said while giggling a little bit.
"But how can you stop this behaviour? How can you make people, what they should be according to you?" she asked.
I smiled and said "That is the point mother, I will not be going to change them, I will just give them information and facts and let themselves decides the best for them," I said.
She was looking confused so I asked
"what happened?"

"Nothing, you just going to give them a random bunch of information while thinking that they will be going to figure it out the way you do? Don't you think that taking them on the right path Is your job?" she said.
The sound of the wind is no better than ever and, at that moment, I know what I really want to say to my mother.
"NO"
She was shocked.
"Mother, I will not be going to lead them anywhere. I will not repeat what had done before"
She asked, "what do you mean by not repeating?"
"I will not repeat what my ancestors had done with their time, they thought that they had founded the perfect cure, in fact in each and every religion someone is there who is considered to be the perfect

person and people around him\her copied them. This must not happen again; I am not a person who says each and everything in perfect order and I know that"

She also stood from her chair while her face transmits fear.

"Do you want to say there is no perfect way and humanity is just on the edge of extinction as a moral force?" she asked.

"NO mother, I couldn't be more wrong if I say those words"

"Then what do you mean son?"

"I mean that there is a way but it is not perfect, it just being better. As humans, we have to accept that at one point the situation around us will change and we have to change according to them, as once said before 'Traditions are changed according to the situations, not the other way around. We have to accept that no matter what traditions we make or break, they all going to have an expiry date on it, with time they will get better or will get vanished. It is the nature of Nature, humans evolved into better once, rivers became oceans, animals evolve and make highbred, even stars turned into drafts or black holes, and even smart ancient people of civilizations also wrote in their writings that 'change and death is inevitable"

She was looking at me while I said all these words, she leaped and kissed my forehead. Even though

she is 5 inches shorter than me, her toes had done a wonderful job.
I came to my senses and asked her.
"Mother, why are you doing this?"
She gave me a confused look "Because I love you. Do I have to ask for your permission before kissing my little boy?" Eyes filled with anger.
"NO NO, I mean, why are you helping me in finding a way out of this so-called traditional problem?" I asked clearly this time.
"oh that" her voice came back to a normal pace and so does the speed of my heartbeat.
It's really strange for me to understand that how can a women's emotions change from being angry to happy in just a second.
"Actually, this is just called a real belief," she said those words and I came back to reality from my own created universe of questions and answers.
"What do you mean by that? You are helping me understand and change the human aspect of religion while considering that my theories about it are true and you think that by doing that you are making your beliefs stronger?"
"YES," she said with the utmost pride she can fill in her eyes.
"But how?" I asked
"Son, do you even attend a court hearing?"
"no, but I saw many on television"

"Yeah, let's imagine that traditions and religion are suspect in a case and there is an investigator who investigates to ease the turmoil and proof them guilty or innocent, if I truly believe in them then I will have no issue if someone will believe in them or not because I know that the truth will prevail in the end and it will be the truth, I practiced my entire life."

"but..." I was about to say something but she cut me off.

"let me finish" she stopped me with her tiny hand.

"oaky," I said.

"good, now I am not saying that you are a police investigator officer, but if I truly believe in my values then I have no problem by someone investigating them, in fact, the people who stopped you from raising question are the real culprit because they think that our or their own religion really lacks something and someone will be going to uncover it, it is there thinking. They think that they are saving the all mighty, but who are they to save someone who made an entire universe by himself. Who are they to think they should protect a tradition which was created by God himself?" anyone who ever lived with humans and has a little knowledge of face reading can now predict that she can kill if someone tried to make her calm, so I don't even dare.

After 20 seconds I guess, I asked “mother, honestly I don’t understand the example of this investigation thing very well”

She looked at me for 3 seconds straight and then a little giggle came out from her mouth.

“oaky, then let me ask you a question. Whose was there to protect a baby?” she asked

“a mother” I replied.

“and who was there to protect us all?” she asked me, guessing that I would come up with the answer she had in her mind.

“We are,” I said simply.

There was clearly disappointment on her face.

“No, you dumbo, the answer is GOD. GOD was there or I should say GOD is here to protect us. The most powerful being.”

“Alright, but what is your point?”

“Do you ever think who is there to protect God?” she asked.

I thought about it and the answer is really simple.

“mother, If the theories of god are true then he doesn’t need protection, Afterall all the weapons, viruses, and anything harmful came to existence after he created the universe.”

“exactly right, there is no one who can harm the all-mighty one because he is the supreme power, the creator, the destroyer, and anything else in between too,” she said while smiling a little.

“oaky, but what is your point mother?” I asked.

She looked at me and without flinching she said. "no one should, or can protect god because protection is for the person who is in a weak state. You will help the poor with food but never help the rich with petrol. You will help a kid who gets injured but never help a bodybuilder to lift kinds of stuff. Even in your favourite superhero movies, the main character will also say 'I am here to protect those who cannot protect themselves either by words or by actions" I was listening to all of this while thinking how enthusiastically she was telling me all this.

"and that is the reason" she continued "why religion don't need a saviour. All the saviours, gods, profits and relatives of all-mighty are gone from the earth and only we are left here to walk on their path of the piece, of course, every now and then some changes are needed on every aspect of things that we do in life, but religion doesn't need protection from us to be present in this world, after all, it is the way of god, and because we are not more powerful than traditions made by our actual saviours we have no right to be called as protectors or contractors of this sacred way of life."

Her words took the form of logical laws created by traditional values, for me.

"We only can take that path and took everyone who joins us in that, as once said by some genius "if an egg is broken from an outside force, a life ends, if it is broken by an inside force, life begins. Great things always begin from the inside."

She wants me to understand her ideology for religious values, and it is true that she never ever forced me to pursue anything beyond my will. She not only say these quotes but uses them in life also.

"son," she said while her eyes met mine "if you don't accept god's way from your heart and doing acting on your side to 'fit in', then you are just manipulating others surrounded by you and that is the far most crime you can do in the territory of god, and that is 'playing with someone's feelings"

"I totally do understand your way mother and I really think it is the right one," I said.

"son, we are no one to decide what is right and what is wrong"

And at this moment I was thinking

'she was right. There is no definition of right and wrong overall, people just live their lives according to their perspectives.'

"We can just follow what our heart says, and deep inside we all know what is right and not, we just learn to hear the voice in our head which comes through our heart" she was looking like a great philosopher, even better than me.

At that moment, i realized that my mother and I were walking on the same path with different modes, we both don't like to force people, we both don't like to manipulate them and we both want to protect our ends.

The wind gets a little speed and because of that utensils started to play with themselves, the voice was not in a pattern but I like it anyway.

Mother was standing there and I don't know back then why? Her eyes filled with tears and her face got a smile, at the same time.

I asked her "what happen, mother? Why are you crying?"

"oh, nothing," she said while rubbing the almost fallen tear of her right eye.

"Tell me, mother"

Without looking at me "I miss your father" she sat down on the chair "he also believed that humanity can only be saved by humans, not gods or profits or relative or gods, but only by humans, today after talking to you, I realized that I miss his teachings and at the top of it. I miss him the most"

I do know that there is no way I can replace my father but I do know the need for this situation.

Without waiting more, I hugged my mother and her tears were flowing right from my shoulder like a river. Her voice did not raise but I can hear her pain. Mother and I were on the same level. We both want to ease our pain by pursuing something that can help us in it.

Mother accepts the path of spirituality, god, and religion to be what she thought is necessary for a better world.
I on the other hand accept science, logic, and moral education to be what I think is necessary for a better world.
We both want to be a shield for innocents and their families, so that the pain we are feeling, must never be felt by others.
I don't know why I don't pursue my mother's teaching or why my mother refuses to be on the logical side, but at that moment we were together, remembering my father.
For the first time maybe in my conscious life, I felt a tear slip from my eye.

CONCLUSION

"So mother, what's next?" after hugging for 10 long emotional minutes I get my powers back of fooling around with jokes.

"Jeff, you have your life and I have mine. I don't want you to be get feared by society and forceful join me on a traditional level, but at the same time, I also don't want to leave anything I put my beliefs in" she said without a flinch.

"then there is nothing we should change; it is our perspective and we should accept it," I said.

"yes, but from time to time you have to came with me to church and mosque, not for me, but for your father," she said while laughing a little.

"yes," I said this yes not because of my father but because of my mother, I don't know for sure that my father will get any kind of benefit from this but I know that the smile on my mother's face will be going to remain on her face.

I know now that we both have differences but we both are ready to understand each other, I know that she and I will not be going to agree on certain things but our bond is surely gotten stronger than before.

we both are smiling looking at each other faces, the chattering of birds is on the run and I am feeling a change of morals in me.

I felt that maybe I don't hate traditions; after all, brushing your teeth, making your bed, studies, jobs all these are one kind of traditions.

It is just the way it is put on us, like a "have to do the thing" in a manner of punishment to born and breath.

This world is full of beautiful, innocent, and good-hearted people who never done anything consciously wrong for their own benefit, and more than enough traditions are there to make them beg for forgiveness without any sin; I don't hate the result as much as I hate the way it is getting done.

But as always, I am not here to judge anyone who is doing this on his own, who is feeling good by doing all these things but we should never make others feel guilty just because their thinking is different than ours.

This should be a teaching in our very first class so that we learn how to accept the most beautiful thing nature offer us: variety.

We have millions of varieties, we have a variety of genders as men and women where both have different mind sets, we have a variety of different law to ease our job. But most importantly we have a variety of perspectives.

Each human being has a set of different experiences with the world around him, what we are today is only due to our memories with our surroundings. It means there are more than 8 billion different perspectives on our planet only.

If we start to accept that people around us are different and the fact that 'we have to face variety in each and every aspect of our lives' then only we can be truly at the piece.

We cannot expect everything to work out according to some plane of ours, but we can accept the situation and can work according to our needs and situation's demand.

We all know lying is a bad thing to do, but lying for saving an innocent life is good. That's how nothing is ideal.

My mother and my beliefs are different but now I know that we will not be going to fight on this topic because we accept each other.

If people around the world start to accept each other and stop putting their own beliefs on someone else for their own peace of mind then this world will become a better place for sure.

We have to start talking with each other, not to say our point only but to listen to someone else's opinion also, even on one of the most sensitive topics of all time.

The storm is itself a variety that we don't expect in our area but by accepting it as it was, we are able to get through it and by accepting our loved once's beliefs we get through our conflict.

No matter what the situation is, we can get through it by actually accepting it, as it is and then making solutions from our ends

"son" she snapped me out of my thinking territory.

"yes mother"

"this Sunday, I will be happier if you can come with me to the church" for the first time in my conscious memory she asked me and not told me to come along with her.

"so do I," I said these words and there was a light on my mother's face, the beautiful light of the sun rising.

I turned my head and witnessed the most amazing sunrise of my life.

Bird's chattering was louder than before, everything else was quiet and peaceful. The wind was heart-warming and the sky was about to coloured up.

The sun was rising and that was the end of our beloved STORMING NIGHT.